Crusty Cupcake's Happy Birthday

Sarviol Publishing
Copyright © Nick Rokicki and Joseph Kelley, 2013

ISBN: 978-1491077535

Special wholesale and re-sale rates are available. For more information,
please contact Deb Harvest at petethepopcorn@gmail.com

When purchasing this book, please consider purchasing
an additional copy to donate to your local library.

Crusty Cupcake's
Happy Birthday!
Friendships Last Forever

3/2014

Books make great gifts!

Nick Rokicki

Thank you

Written by **Nick Rokicki** & **Joseph Kelley**
Illustrated by **Ronaldo Florendo**

This book is dedicated, in loving memory, to
Abigail Teague.

The cupcakes at Queen Nom Nom's Cupcake Factory just loved celebrating birthdays ... which happened often, considering that cupcakes were born every day!

Paisley the Peanut Butter and Jelly Cupcake clapped as the other cupcakes finished their song. "Thank you all very much," came the cool comment from Paisley's lips, "but I just cannot wait to open my gifts!"

Paisley wasn't a very patient cupcake. While the other cupcakes were **celebrating**, she began snooping around the shop, looking for her gifts!

Maybe under the colored kiddie table?
Hmmm... not there.

Palmer the Pumpkin Cupcake looked at Penny the Peach Cupcake...

who looked at
**Sampson the Strawberry
Cupcake...**

who looked at
Bailey the Blueberry
Cupcake...

who looked at
Reggie the Root Beer Cupcake...

who looked at
Holly the Hot Fudge
Cupcake...

who looked at
**Salvador the S'more
Cupcake...**

"Gifts! Paisley the Peanut Butter and Jelly Cupcake is expecting gifts for her birthday," explained Reggie to Roxie. What could the cupcakes do?

"I'm waiting..." said **Paisley**, tapping her toes on the table.

"Here! Here! Happy Birthday," said Penny as she passed Paisley a piece of her peach.

"Birthdays are beautiful," blared **Bailey**, bouncing a **blueberry** toward **Paisley**.

"Have a swirl of this bright new frosting," came the comment from **Palmer**, holding a tub of gooey topping.

"Sweet strawberry for
the sweet birthday girl,"
said **Sampson** as he stretched
to give **Paisley** a strawberry.

Paisley wasn't pleased. "I don't want pieces of cupcakes or wrappings or frostings for my birthday! I want jewelry and video games and a phone and money! Your gifts don't mean anything!"

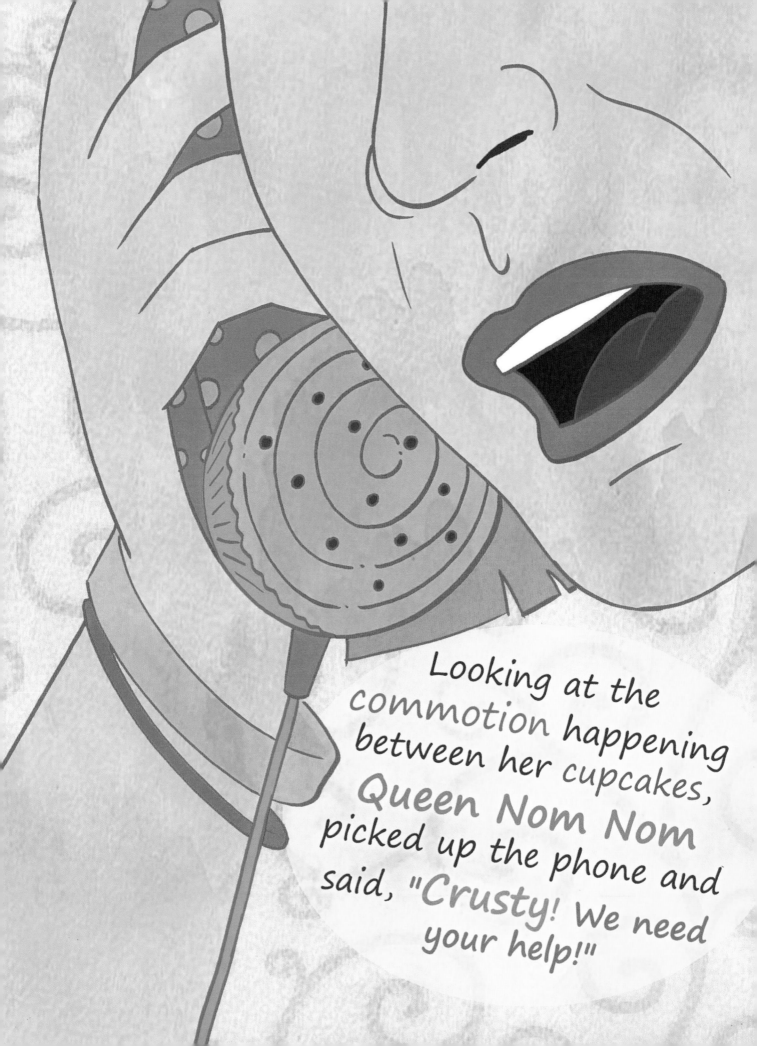

Looking at the commotion happening between her cupcakes, Queen Nom Nom picked up the phone and said, "Crusty! We need your help!"

As fast as you can spell frosting, wise old **Crusty the Carrot Cupcake** entered the shop, saying, "Calm! Calm! You **cupcakes** don't have to cry! All of you were being very good friends to young **Paisley**. It was **generous** of you to offer her something for her **birthday**... but you've already given her the greatest gift there is," said **Crusty**.

"Gift? They didn't give me any gifts at all!" puffed Paisley.

Paisley peered at the proud cupcakes surrounding her.

Crusty was right... all of these cupcakes were her friends. She was too focused on gifts, rather than feeling gratitude for the good times and laughs she could have been having at her party.

"I'm sorry, everyone! Let's just have fun--- and have a real birthday party," said **Paisley**.

With that, **Crusty** started singing, "Happy Birthday to you! Happy birthday to you!"

Soon, all of the **cupcakes** joined in and celebrated the birthday of their new friend, **Paisley Brooke Jackson**, the **Peanut Butter** and **Jelly Cupcake**!

HAPPY BIRTHDAY!

HAPPY BIRTHDAY!

A Note...
from Nick and Joe

First, thanks for picking up this book. Reading is the most vital skill you will need to sail the waters of life. Speaking of sailing, we thought we'd like to talk to you, here at the end of this story, about adventure. If there is one thing that is guaranteed in life, it's adventure. You'll see plenty of ups and downs. You will meet new people every day. Some of you will travel the world. Others will find your happiness right where you grew up. All of this is part of the grandest adventure that we call life.

We've learned that the biggest adventures happen when you are helping other people. Over the past couple of years, we have read our first book **Pete the Popcorn** to over 100,000 school children in over 25 states. This tour was funded completely through sales of our books and our own personal savings. It was important to accomplish this, to get children excited about reading... and to teach them how one simple act of saying something nice to someone else, can positively change the world.

Another prominent lesson is gratitude. In **Crusty Cupcake's Happy Birthday**, young Paisley Brooke Jackson learns that the real gift is having all of her friends present to celebrate her birthday. This is a lesson we can all think about daily. Look around. What are you truly grateful for?

We once heard that experiences are greater than possessions. The experiences that we've had: meeting thousands of children and parents, contributing to other organizations promoting literacy, partnering with local businesses that are looking to make a positive impact on their community through literature... We would absolutely agree that experiences are greater than possessions. Go out and give— find your experience.

Finally, whenever it is, Happy Birthday! On your birthday, take a moment and think about gratitude... and then make a wish, blow out the candle and eat that cupcake!

-Nick and Joe

Friendships last forever... the authors, with a group of friends on one of their adventures.

The authors, pictured at one of their hundreds of school visits across the country.

Joe Kelley and Nick Rokicki, pictured with Toure McCord, founder of Books 4 Buddies.

Nom Nom's Cupcake Factory is based in Michigan, with their flagship location in Westland, the hometown of co-author Joe Kelley.

Daily, Nom Nom's offers countless varieties of cupcakes, meeting high standards of freshness, quality and CREATIVITY! Try Twin Chocolate Temptation... or Caramel Pretzel... or Maple Bacon... or any of the nearly 100 flavors on the menu!

Mother and Daughter owners Laura Wier and Jennifer Ryan are committed to raising childhood literacy rates across the country... and what better way than through cupcakes? Learn more at www.queennomnoms.com

Kids Love Nom Nom's!!!

Ronaldo Florendo

After completing this third project with Nick and Joe, illustrator Ronald Florendo is hard at work on a few more projects slated for 2014. While not making cupcakes come alive, Ron enjoys his time playing the bass guitar. To learn more, visit www.Behance.net/RMFlorendo14

#ENCOURAGE

Pete the Popcorn is a nationally recognized book for children that promotes a lesson of encouragement over bullying. Pete is a popcorn kernel, struggling with popping up. Not feeling too peppy, Pete's friend Patty offers him words of encouragement. Kids learn that a kind word goes a long way! www.Facebook.com/PeteThePopcorn

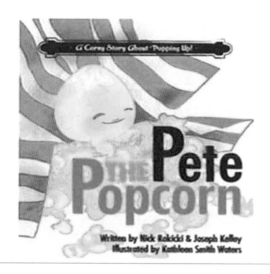

#FAMILY

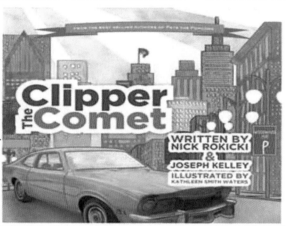

Come for a cruise in Clipper the Comet! This vocabulary-building book will delight children and car lovers of all ages. Featuring a *real* 1975 Mercury Comet, the book teaches kids the valuable lesson of working hard and taking pride in your family. www.Facebook.com/ClipperTheComet

#ACCEPTANCE

Casey and Callie Cupcake is a Frosted Fable About Being Fantastic... Just The Way You Are! "I'm better than you are!" and "No you're not!" have been the start of many arguments. In this book, Casey and Callie learn important lessons from Crusty the Carrot Cupcake! Teaching children to accept themselves & others for who they are on the inside!

www.Facebook.com/CupcakeBook

#SMILE

While on their Encouragement Across America Tour in 2012, authors Nick Rokicki and Joe Kelley asked teachers how kids could encourage other kids. Their answer always included the word "Smile!" So, First Photo of The Royal Baby teaches this lesson in a heartwarming fashion... while having a bit of fun with Her Majesty!

www.Facebook.com/RoyalBabyPhoto

Upcoming Releases

Gilbert the Grasshopper is the highly-anticipated book from Nick Rokicki and Joe Kelley. Slated for release on March 3rd, 2014, Gilbert is the tale of an overly curious grasshopper who learns lessons in one very exciting day. Fortunately for a new friend, Gilbert is ready and willing to share his newfound knowledge with others!

PLUS...

Pete the Popcorn is popping up for **PART TWO** on **January 19th, 2014!** Celebrate National Popcorn Day with your favorite little kernel!

Special Thanks

FOR SUPPORTING LITERACY IN LOCAL SCHOOLS

Made in the USA
Charleston, SC
22 September 2015